There's a Hurricane in the Pool!

by **Jessica Gunderson**
illustrated by **Jorge Santillan**

STONE ARCH BOOKS
a capstone imprint

VICTORY SCHOOL SUPERSTARS

Sports Illustrated KIDS *There's a Hurricane in the Pool!*
is published by Stone Arch Books — A Capstone Imprint
151 Good Counsel Drive, P.O. Box 669
Mankato, Minnesota 56002
www.capstonepub.com

Art Director and Designer: Bob Lentz
Creative Director: Heather Kindseth
Production Specialist: Michelle Biedscheid

Timeline photo credits: Library of Congress (middle left);
Shutterstock/C. Byatt-Norman (top right), Gualtiero Boffi
(top left);Sports Illustrated/Heinz Kluetmeier (bottom),
Simon Bruty (middle right).

Library of Congress Cataloging-in-Publication Data is
available on the Library of Congress website.

ISBN: 978-1-4342-2230-5 (library binding)
ISBN: 978-1-4342-3078-2 (paperback)

Summary: Kenzie's strength creates huge waves in the pool,
while her temper creates even bigger trouble.

Printed in the United States of America in Stevens Point, Wisconsin.
092010   005934WZS11

TABLE of CONTENTS

Kenzie Winz

Swimming

AGE: 10
GRADE: 4
SUPER SPORTS ABILITY: Super strength

VICTORY SCHOOL SUPERSTARS

CARMEN   ALICIA   JOSH   DANNY   KENZIE   TYLER

VICTORY SCHOOL MAP

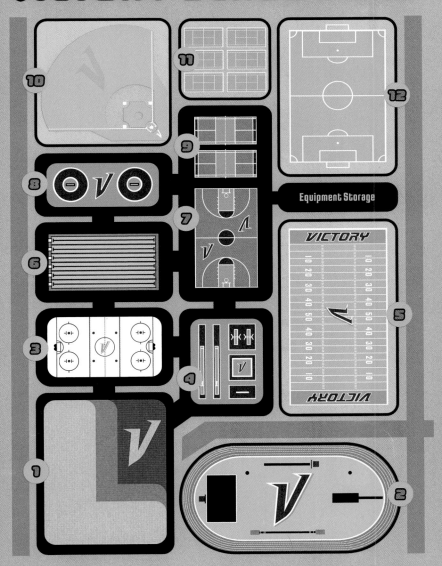

Equipment Storage

VICTORY

VICTORY

1. **Main Offices/Classrooms**
2. **Track and Field**
3. **Hockey/Figure Skating**
4. **Gymnastics**
5. **Football**
6. **Swimming**
7. **Basketball**
8. **Wrestling**
9. **Volleyball**
10. **Baseball/Softball**
11. **Tennis**
12. **Soccer**

CHAPTER 1

Super Strength

I am dripping wet and shivering.

"I hate swimming class," I grumble to my friend Josh. He's standing next to me on the deck of the pool. He's shivering too.

"I know, Kenzie," Josh says. "You've told me that before. Like five minutes ago."

"Sorry," I say. "It's just that my strength—"

A whistle blows, interrupting me. It's Ms. Stanford, our swimming teacher. That whistle means that we should jump back into the pool. I plug my nose and jump in.

"Say, Ms. Stanford," Josh calls, "can we jump off the high dive today?"

"If there's time," Ms. Stanford promises.

"I hope so!" exclaim Kim and Tim together. Kim and Tim are twins, and their special skill is synchronized diving. They can perform exactly the same dives at exactly the same time. Even their splashes are identical.

Ms. Stanford tells us to swim the front crawl. Ugh! The front crawl is the worst. I can never get the breathing rhythm right. I usually end up sucking in a lung full of water.

Ms. Stanford twirls her whistle and looks down at me. She says, "And remember, Kenzie—"

"Control my strength," I finish.

I've been hearing those words ever since I discovered my super strength. When I was three years old, I lifted the couch up with one hand so my mom could vacuum under it. My family was shocked!

But even then I had more strength than I knew what to do with. I lifted the couch so high, it broke the ceiling fan. "Control your strength," Mom had shouted over the noisy vacuum.

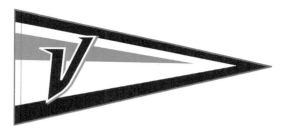

Here at Victory School for Super Athletes, it's usually my gymnastics coach telling me to have more control. I am a gymnast. But even during a sport I love, I have trouble controlling my super strength. Once I even broke the balance beam.

"Use steady, even kicks, just below the surface of the water," Ms. Stanford reminds us. "Keep your legs straight and feet floppy."

She blows the whistle, and I push off from the side of the pool. Every second arm rotation, I lilt my head for air.

I reach the other side of the pool without choking on water once. Maybe I'm getting the hang of this swimming thing.

I wipe the water from my eyes and look around me.

Or, maybe not.

Giant waves rise and break against the side of the pool. Kim and Tim are rubbing their heads. I guess they were knocked together by the strong waves. All the other kids are glaring at me. And so is Ms. Stanford.

I know why. I am the one who caused the waves. I kicked so hard it sent waves around the pool.

Josh emerges next to me. "I might have to start calling you The Wavemaker," he says. "It's like there's a hurricane in the pool!"

"I told you I hate swimming," I say.

He shrugs and says, "It's not my favorite either. I prefer frozen water."

Josh is a champion figure skater. He has perfect footwork on the ice. Figure skating isn't his only sport, though. He's also great at hockey.

The bell rings, and we get out of the pool. Josh looks at the high dive. "I really wanted to dive today," he says.

I wrap myself in a towel and try to hide from the other students' glares.

"How do you do it, Josh?" I moan. "How do you control your skill? Don't your feet always want to do fancy footwork?"

Josh rubs his hair with his towel. "I admit," he says, "swimming takes more concentration than skating."

"I'd rather just do gymnastics all the time," I say.

Josh nods. "For me, ice skating is so easy I don't have to think about it," he says. "For others, skating takes a lot of practice. Remember the first time Danny tried to skate?"

I giggle at the memory. Danny, a
football player, is the fastest kid at Victory.
Once he tried to ice skate just like Josh.
He thought he'd be faster than Josh, even
though he'd never ice skated before.

But his feet moved so fast that the ice melted in ridges. Instead of speed skating, he fell down.

"I remember," I say. "But he's good now!"

"Yeah," Josh agrees. "He can almost outskate me!"

"I guess it just takes practice," I admit. "But I don't want to learn to swim. When will I ever need to swim? I'm a gymnast!"

As I head to swim class the next day, I think about what Josh said. It is true. Some people lift weights their entire lives just to have strength like mine. Learning to swim will take some work.

I sit down on the edge of the pool, my feet hanging in the water. Next to me, Kim and Tim, the twins, are whispering. I can tell they are talking about me.

When Ms. Stanford walks onto the deck to begin class, Kim stands up. "If Kenzie is in the pool, I don't want to swim," she complains.

"Yesterday our heads bumped together from all her waves," Tim agrees, rubbing the side of his head.

I look down at my feet sloshing in the pool, but not before I see the other kids nodding in agreement.

"I like swimming with Kenzie," Josh defends. "And by the way, Tim, it was the other side of your head."

Tim looks embarrassed, and Kim glares at Josh.

"Say, Ms. Stanford," Josh says, "can we jump off the high dive today?"

Ms. Stanford ignores him and strides toward me. "Kenzie, I know you can control your strength. I've told you time and again. You just aren't trying," she adds.

"I am trying," I protest, but maybe she's right.

Ms. Stanford crosses her arms.

I sigh. "Swimming is just so hard for me," I whine. "There's so much to remember. And I'm a gymnast! I don't need to know how to swim."

Ms. Stanford's glare deepens, and her crossed arms cross even tighter. "You don't, huh?" she says.

"When will I ever need to know the front crawl, or the butterfly, or the backstroke?" I continue. "I can float and doggie paddle. That's all I need."

But I am not convincing Ms. Stanford. From her expression, I can tell that I'm going to be in deep trouble — unless I can swim a lap without causing too many waves.

I'll try, I tell myself.

Trouble

At Ms. Stanford's whistle, I push off from the side of the pool and glide into the water. I can hear her coaching the kids around me. "Keep your legs straight! Slice the water with your hands, don't slap it!"

But she doesn't say anything to me. I smile into the water. Then I realize I'm behind the others. Far, far behind.

This isn't a race, but at Victory we are all athletes. That means we are competitive, even in sports we don't care about. Like swimming.

There's only one thing I can do to catch up. I pound my legs into the water with all my strength. I feel waves building with the power of my kick. But I don't care.

My fingers touch the wall. I lift my head from the water and grin as I look around me. Everyone is clutching the side of the pool as waves knock against them. They are trying to catch their breath. Water is even dripping from the walls.

"Sorry," I say. My grin vanishes.

And then I look at Josh. He is staring past my shoulder in horror.

"What?" I ask.

I turn, following his gaze, and then I see. "Uh-oh," I say.

A giant wave is rolling toward the edge of the pool. Ms. Stanford is right in its path.

"Look out!" I shout, but it's too late. The wave crashes onto the deck, knocking Ms. Stanford off her feet.

Her whistle goes flying. Her clipboard goes flying. Her eyes and mouth pop into Os of surprise, but then they quickly close into lines of anger. "Kenzie!" she shouts.

"Sorry Ms. Stanford," I say. "But did you see? I was controlling my strength. Until I lagged behind."

Ms. Stanford shakes her head. Drops of water fly from her hair. She is soaking wet. "You can do your explaining in my office. After school," she says.

"But I have gymnastics practice!"
I protest.

I can tell Ms. Stanford is not going to budge. I climb out of the pool. My eyes burn with anger, tears, and chlorine. I stomp past the eyes of the other kids. I stomp past Ms. Stanford, without offering to help her up. I stomp past the high dive.

And then I make a big mistake. I kick the cement pole of the high dive.

The High Dive

Kicking the pole may not seem like a big deal. And it wouldn't be, for kids with normal strength. But I kick with all the anger and energy inside me.

I don't think about what will happen. I just keep stomping toward the locker room.

And then I hear a *CRRAACCCK!*
Shocked gasps erupt from the other kids.
Ms. Stanford blows her never-ending
whistle.

I turn just in time to see the high
dive teetering. A million little cracks are
splintering the pole right where I kicked it.

Kids are jumping out of the pool and scurrying away.

"Timber!" someone shouts.

"No, not the high dive!" Josh groans just as the dive topples forward into the water. It floats for a moment and then sinks with a slow slurp.

I turn around and keep stomping toward the locker room.

"How are we going to get it out?" moans Tim.

"No one is strong enough," adds Kim.

There's a pause, and then they both exclaim, "Kenzie!"

But I don't stop. I keep stomping into the locker room to grab my clothes, and then I stomp into the hall. I hear my name again.

This time it's Josh.

CHAPTER 6

Handy Skills

"I'm not going back," I tell him.

He looks at me sadly. "Please? You're the only one strong enough to help!" he says.

"No," I say.

"But Kenzie, I really wanted to jump off the high dive," he pleads. "Now I'll never be able to."

"Someone else will fix it," I say.

"But it will take forever to get a new high dive!" he says. "By then, we'll be done with the swimming unit."

He has a point.

"Oh, all right," I say.

As I follow him back into the pool area, he says, "Now don't throw another temper tantrum."

"I don't throw tantrums!" I yell.

Josh laughs at me, and I realize how loud my voice is.

"You're right," I say, laughing too. "I do throw tantrums. I guess I need to control my anger just like I need to control my strength."

In the pool area, everyone is staring into the water at the sunken diving board. I'm sure they aren't too happy with me, but all I can do is try to make things right. I take a deep breath and get ready to plunge into the water. Just then, there's a tap on my shoulder.

Uh-oh. It's Ms. Stanford. And she doesn't look happy.

"I guess your swimming skills are coming in handy, huh?" she says.

I can't help but smile. "I guess you're right, Ms. Stanford," I say.

And then I dive in.

GLOSSARY

chlorine (KLOR-een)—a gas that is added to water to kill harmful germs

competitive (kuhm-PET-uh-tiv)—very eager to win

concentration (kon-suhn-TRAY-shun)—focused thoughts and attention on something

expression (ek-SPRESH-uhn)—the look on someone's face

gymnastics (jim-NASS-tiks)—physical exercises, often performed on special equipment, that involve careful and exact body movements

hurricane (HUR-uh-kane)—a violent sea storm with high winds

interrupting (in-tuh-RUHPT-ing)—to start talking or making a noise before someone else has finished talking

rhythm (RITH-uhm)—a regular beat

rotation (roh-TAY-shun)—a turn around a fixed point

synchronized (SING-kruh-nized)—happening at the same time

tantrums (TAN-truhms)—outbursts of anger

SWIMMING IN HISTORY

9000 B.C. Paintings of swimmers are made on cave walls in Libya.

36 A.D. Swim races are recorded in **Japan.**

1538 *Art of Swimming* is published in Europe.

1875 Captain Matthew Webb becomes the first person to swim across the English Channel. He swims it in 21 hours and 45 minutes.

1896 Swimming is part of the first modern **Olympics.**

1926 American **Gertrude Ederle** becomes the first woman to swim the English Channel. It takes her 14 hours and 30 minutes.

1964 Fourteen-year-old Lillian "Pokey" Watson becomes the youngest American to win an Olympic swimming medal.

1972 Mark Spitz sets seven world records as he wins seven gold medals in the Olympics.

1987 Fifteen-year-old **Janet Evans** breaks three world records.

2008 American swimmer **Michael Phelps** becomes the star of the Olympics with his eight gold medals.

THE ALLTIME OLYMPIAN MICHAEL PHELPS

Sports Illustrated

VICTORY SCHOOL SUPERSTARS

Five Fouls and You're Out!

It's a Wrestling Mat, Not a Dance Floor

There's a Hurricane in the Pool!

There's No Crying in Baseball

Who Wants to Play Just for Kicks?

You Can't Spike Your Serves

Read them ALL!